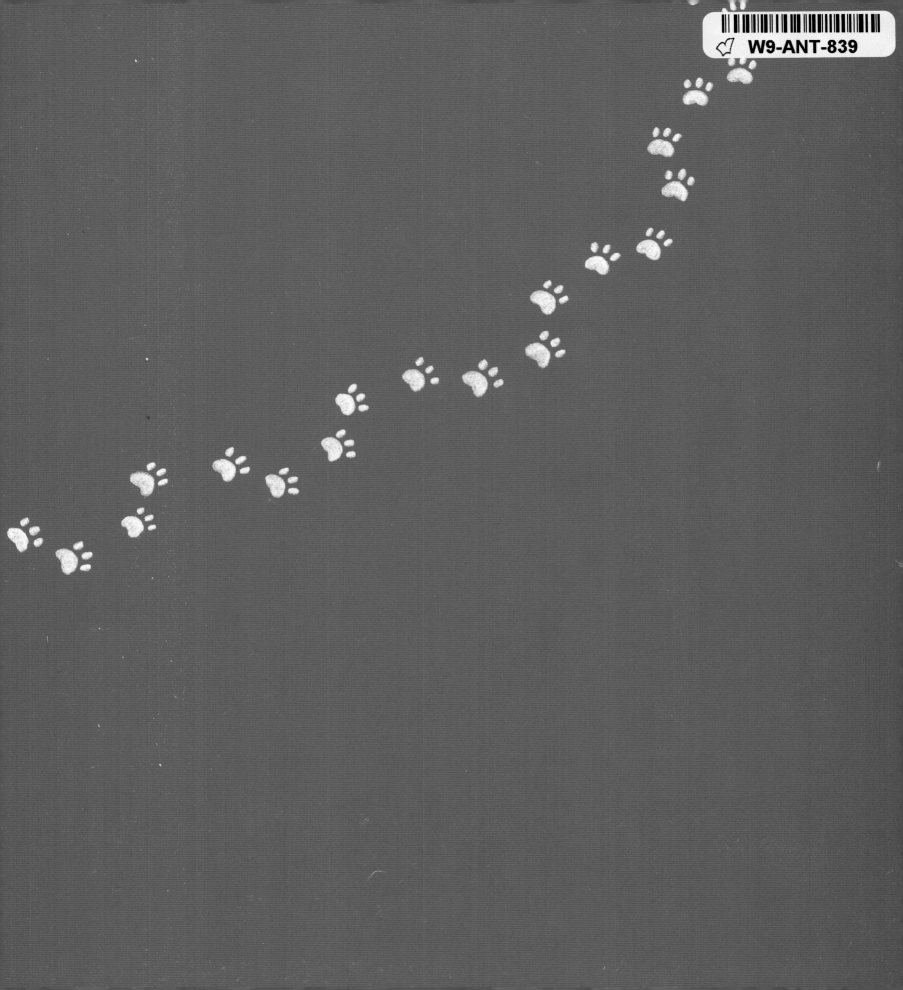

A HOP IS UP

Kristy Dempsey

illustrated by Lori Richmond

BLOOMSBURY

NEW YORK LONDON OXFORD NEW DELHI SYDNEY

First published in the United States of America in September 2016
by Bloomsbury Children's Books
www.bloomsbury.com

Bloomsbury is a registered trademark of Bloomsbury Publishing Plc

For information about permission to reproduce selections from this book, write to
Permissions, Bloomsbury Children's Books, 1385 Broadway, New York, New York 10018
Bloomsbury books may be purchased for business or promotional use. For information on bulk
purchases please contact Macmillan Corporate and Premium Sales Department at
specialmarkets@macmillan.com

Library of Congress Cataloging-in-Publication Data
Names: Dempsey, Kristy. | Richmond, Lori, illustrator.
Title: A hop is up / by Kristy Dempsey ; illustrated by Lori Richmond.
Description: New York : Bloomsbury, 2016.
Summary: Walking with his energetic puppy in their neighborhood, a young boy hops, bends, spins,
and jumps with friends he encounters along the way.
Identifiers: LCCN 2015040006
ISBN 978-1-61963-390-2 (hardcover) • ISBN 978-1-68119-071-6 (board)
Subjects: | CYAC: Stories in rhyme. | Play–Fiction. | BISAC: JUVENILE FICTION/Concepts/Sounds. |
JUVENILE FICTION/Concepts/Words. | JUVENILE FICTION/Imagination & Play.
Classification: LCC PZ8.3.D4315 Ho 2016 | DDC [E]–dc23
LC record available at http://lccn.loc.gov/2015040006

Art created with ink and watercolors and composited digitally
Typeset in Burbank Big Wide Medium
Book design by John Candell
Printed in China by Leo Paper Products, Heshan, Guangdong
1 3 5 7 9 10 8 6 4 2

For Libby, Selena, and Ava: I'd hop across
the world for you! —K. D.

For my mom and dad, who encouraged me
to leap. —L. R.

A hop is UP.

A bend is **DOWN.**

A spin is AROUND
and AROUND
and AROUND.

A jump is OVER,

from here

to there.

A **LEAP** repeats
when there's a pair.

A march is
RIGHT-LEFT,
RIGHT-LEFT,
RIGHT.

A jig's a
WIGGLY,
GIGGLY
sight.

A slip's a **SLIDE.**

A slide's a **SLIP.**

A BOING-BOING-BOING

is a SKIP-SKIP-SKIP.

A swing is **UP** and **OUT**, and then . . .
back and **UP** and **OUT** again.

A walk is
AMBLE-
RAMBLE-
SLOW.

A race is a **RUN**,
so go, go, **GO!**

A finish is an **END**,

a pause is a **WAIT**.

A rest is a STOP...

but a hop . . .

...is UP!